Bramble and Berry

The fox cub peered nervously through the long grass. He stared at the kitten's dark, stripy face and her long white whiskers. He had been watching her for a while. She looked very fierce, especially when she had pounced on that piece of straw. *Please don't pounce on me too*, the cub thought, trembling with fear . . .

Jenny Dale's Best Friends

More Best Friends follow soon!

Best ♥ Friends

Bramble and Berry

by Jenny Dale

Illustrated by Susan Hellard

A Working Partners Book

MACMILLAN CHILDREN'S BOOKS

Special thanks to Jill Atkins

First published in 2002 by Macmillan Children's Books
a division of Macmillan Publishers Limited
20 New Wharf Road, London N1 9RR
Basingstoke and Oxford
www.panmacmillan.com

Associated companies throughout the world

Created by Working Partners Limited
London W6 0QT

ISBN 0 330 39857 1

5 7 9 8 6 4

A CIP catalogue record for this book is available from
the British Library.

Typeset by SX Composing DTP, Rayleigh, Essex
Printed and bound in Great Britain by Mackays of Chatham plc, Kent

chapter one

"Look at me!" Bramble dug her sharp claws into the wooden beam, high in the barn. She peered down at her mum, Tabitha.

"Bramble, come down at once," mewed Tabitha. "You'll fall!"

"But it's such fun up here," the kitten miaowed. "I can see lots of exciting things!" She loved looking up at the birds' nests high in the eaves. And she could even see mice scuttling about among the bales of straw below.

"It's all right, Mum," she purred. "I'm quite safe."

At that moment, Bramble felt her paws slipping. She tried to dig her claws deeper. Too late! "Oops!" she wailed as she fell.

The air whistled through Bramble's whiskers and ruffled her furry coat. Halfway down, Bramble flipped her body the right way up and landed paws first in a deep pile of straw.

Tabitha trotted over to her. "You must be more careful," she miaowed, giving Bramble a lick. "You'll get into real trouble one day."

Bramble loved the feel of her mum's rough tongue rasping over her face. "Don't worry about me," she purred.

She lifted her head so Tabitha could reach under her chin.

When Tabitha had finished, Bramble leaped up and scampered out into the farmyard. It was a breezy day. A piece of straw blew along the ground in front of her. Bramble pounced on it, feeling it crackle under her front paws.

A sharp gust of wind blew the straw just out of reach. It fluttered away across the yard.

"Come back," Bramble hissed, bounding after it.

Suddenly, she stopped. A pair of dark, shiny eyes stared at her from the long grass at the edge of the yard.

Bramble crept a little nearer. She saw a thin, red face, a shiny, black nose and two very pointed ears.

It was a fox!

Bramble stood very still. She remembered what her mum had taught her. "Foxes are very dangerous. You must run away if you ever see one."

Shaking all over, Bramble began to back away slowly. She hoped the fox

would not come after her.

The fox cub peered nervously through the long grass. He stared at the kitten's dark, stripy face and her long, white whiskers. He had been watching her for a while. She looked very fierce, especially when she had pounced on that piece of straw. *Please don't pounce on me, too*, the cub thought, trembling with fear.

Bramble noticed the grass quivering. The fox was shivering. "Is he frightened of *me*?" she wondered. Bramble narrowed her eyes and took a closer look. "He's very small," she miaowed. "I'm not scared of *him*!"

Feeling very brave, she stepped forward, arched her back and hissed loudly. "Go away, fox!" she spat.

"Help!" whined the cub. In a panic, he dashed out of the long grass, past the kitten and across the farmyard.

Bramble saw a flash of red fur as the tiny fox shot by. Then she blinked. The fox had disappeared. "I frightened a fox!" she miaowed in surprise.

Bramble scampered to the farmhouse. She stood on her hind legs and pushed her head through the cat flap. "Mum!" she mewed. "I frightened a fox. I scared it right away!"

"A fox?" miaowed Tabitha anxiously, hurrying towards her. "Are you all right?"

"Oh yes," Bramble purred proudly. "We won't see him round here again!"

The fox cub headed for the barn. It was gloomy inside, but he could see a pile of straw in one corner. It would be a good place to hide. He dived into the straw and lay there panting and shaking.

There were strange noises all around him, rustling and fluttering. His heart thumped. He huddled down in the straw, hoping that his mum would come and find him very soon.

Suddenly, the fox cub heard another sound. From his hiding place, he saw a boy enter the barn and walk towards the pile of straw.

"Hello!" said the boy. "There's something hiding in here."

The little fox whined. He pushed his nose deeper into the straw and closed his eyes, hoping the boy wouldn't come any closer. But then he felt a hand stroking his back.

"I don't believe it!" said the boy. "It's a fox cub."

The cub felt the boy's hands lifting him up. He was too frightened to struggle. "Help!" he whimpered.

"Poor thing," said the boy, kindly.

"Are you lost? Don't worry, I'll look after you. I'd better take you indoors."

The boy's quiet voice comforted the fox. He didn't feel quite so scared as the boy carried him out of the barn.

A woman was standing at the farmhouse door. "Hi, Mark," she called. "What have you got there?"

"A fox cub," the boy replied. "Can I keep him?"

The woman hurried over. "He's very tiny," she said. "He'll need careful looking after until we find his mum." She took the cub and stroked him.

The fox cub was not shaking quite so much now. These people had gentle hands and voices. Maybe they would take him back to his mum. He snuggled

into the woman's jumper as she carried
him into the farmhouse. Then he
pricked up his ears and stared around,
his eyes wide. He was in a big room,
which was cool and quiet after the hot,
dusty farmyard.

The woman put the fox down on a soft
blanket. She filled a bowl with water and

put it beside him. The cub looked at the water. He was really thirsty. Slowly, he crept forward to the bowl and began to drink.

Bramble was tucking into some crunchy biscuits when Mark and Mrs Gates came in. Out of the corner of her eye, she spotted a bushy, red tail. She stopped eating and watched the fox cub drink some water.

"What's *he* doing in here?" she hissed. "I thought I got rid of him."

"I think I'll call him Berry," she heard Mark say.

"Berry suits him," said Mrs Gates. "He's the right colour."

Bramble jumped up. "I'm going to frighten that fox away again!" she miaowed. She began to gallop across the kitchen.

Berry saw the stripy-faced creature racing towards him. "Oh no!" he whined. "Here comes that fierce cat again!"

chapter 2

"What are you doing here?" Bramble
hissed. She arched her back.

Berry pressed his nose into the
blanket. "Please don't hurt me," he
whined.

Bramble felt confused as she looked at
the trembling fox. She didn't know what
her mum was making such a fuss was
about. Foxes weren't scary at all!

Tabitha came and stood behind
Bramble. "Well!" she miaowed. "So this
is the fox you frightened away!"

"Yes, Mum," Bramble purred proudly.

"I hadn't realized it was so small," mewed Tabitha.

Bramble rubbed her head against her mum's face. "Aren't all foxes like this, then?" she asked.

"Oh, no," Tabitha replied. "Grown-up foxes are much bigger. This is only a very young cub. No wonder he's scared."

Berry wanted to hide from the stripy-faced kitten. And there was an even *bigger* cat with her. He tugged at the blanket and tried to wriggle underneath it. The edge of the blanket twitched. In a flash, the kitten pounced on it and began to drag the blanket off him.

Berry growled, "Let go!" He grabbed

the other end between his teeth and
pulled. The more Berry pulled at one
end, the harder the kitten tugged at the
other.

Finally, Berry gave up. He lay still,
panting heavily, his heart pounding in
his chest. "I want my mum," he
whimpered sadly.

The kitten came and sat down beside

him. "Why don't you want to play with me?" she miaowed.

At that moment, the woman hurried over and stroked the kitten. "Now then, Bramble, you fierce little monster," she said. "Leave our visitor alone."

The kitten purred and rubbed her head against the woman's hand. Then she trotted away.

Berry sniffed and sat up. What was that delicious smell? He crouched down as the boy loomed over him and put a dish on the floor. Berry sniffed again. He didn't know what was in the dish, but it smelled very tasty! He stepped forward and took a mouthful. Yum! He gulped down all the food and then had another drink of water.

After that he felt much better. He crept
back to the blanket and lay on his side
with his tail stretched out across the
floor. He could keep an eye on the two
cats from there. They were eating some
food as well.

Bramble had nearly finished. She
watched Berry over the top of her dish.
"You look a bit lonely," she mewed. She

quickly washed her whiskers, then jumped up and scampered across the room towards the fox cub.

Berry's heart beat faster as he watched the kitten racing towards him. What was she going to do this time? To his surprise, Bramble stopped, reached out her paw and tapped the tip of his tail.

Berry jumped up and swished his tail behind him. "What are you doing?" he yapped crossly.

But Bramble didn't answer. Instead, she gently patted his nose. Berry blinked, then he tried to pat Bramble back. But she dodged away and raced across the kitchen.

"Come back!" Berry called.

"I bet you can't catch me!" miaowed

Bramble playfully.

Berry set off after Bramble. He tried to catch up with her as she scampered under the table, but it wasn't easy. His paws skidded on the slippery floor. It wasn't like the soft ground in the woods where he lived.

Berry chased Bramble round and round the kitchen, sliding around corners and bumping into the table legs. His ears flapped madly and his tail streamed out behind him. The faster he ran, the more excited he got. This was fun!

Suddenly, Bramble stopped. Berry crashed into her with a bump. They fell over and landed in a heap.

Berry looked at Bramble. She wasn't at

all scary, really. She was soft and furry, and she was out of breath, just like him.

Bramble sat up. "I'm thirsty," she mewed. "Do you want a drink?"

"Yes, I do," yapped Berry.

They trotted to the water bowl and, side by side, they began to lap the cool water.

chapter 3

That night, Berry curled up on his
blanket. He tried hard to get to sleep,
but strange humming and clicking noises
kept him awake. He missed his mum
and his den in the woods, and he
whimpered quietly in the darkness.
Luckily, he could hear Bramble and
Tabitha purring. It made him feel
better to know that Bramble was nearby.
She might even help him find his mum
in the morning. Berry started to feel
sleepy at last.

As soon as it was light, Bramble leaped over the side of the basket and bounded across the kitchen floor. "Berry!" she mewed as she skidded to a halt in front of the blanket. "Are you awake?"

There was no reply, so Bramble craned her neck over the edge of the blanket. She saw a bundle of red fur, two pointed ears and a nose tucked under a white-tipped tail. Berry was fast asleep.

"Come on, lazy bones!" Bramble miaowed, more loudly. "I'm ready to play."

Berry blinked and sat up, looking at Bramble with his head on one side. He yawned. He didn't feel like playing yet. He still felt very sleepy.

Bramble leaped on to the blanket, bounced off again and raced across the floor, but Berry didn't move. Bramble scampered back and began tugging a corner of the blanket. "It's time to play," she miaowed.

Berry slowly stood up and stretched. He watched Bramble scamper over to a little yellow ball. She tapped it so it rolled towards Berry, then she chased it and tapped it again. The ball rolled temptingly across the smooth floor.

Berry bounded off the blanket and raced after the ball. He snatched it up in his mouth, then he shook his head and the ball flew in the air. But as he ran after it again, he felt Bramble's paws grab him. He tumbled on to his side with a grunt.

Bramble pounced on him again and they rolled over and over together on the kitchen floor. She could feel Berry's tickly fur under her paws. She playfully batted his ears, keeping her claws tucked in. "I told you I was going to cheer you up," she panted. "Come on. I'll show you what else we can do."

The door into the sitting room was open. Bramble squeezed through the gap and trotted boldly over to the curtains. "Watch this!" she mewed, digging her claws into the thick, soft material. Up and up she climbed, until Berry looked like a tiny ball of red fluff far below. Suddenly, the door opened and Mrs Gates and Mark came in.

"Bramble!" exclaimed Mrs Gates, lifting her down. "You'll ruin my curtains, you wicked kitten."

But Bramble wasn't listening. She gave a big wriggle and jumped out of Mrs Gates's arms. As soon as her paws touched the carpet, she raced off with Berry close behind her. There was a lovely, thick rug on the other side of the room. It had fluffy tassels on one end. Bramble loved playing with them. She sprang on to the tassels and pulled.

Berry crouched next to her and tugged a tassel hard with his teeth.

"Bramble!" called Mark, laughing and clapping his hands. "Stop teaching Berry all your naughty tricks." He shooed them away from the rug, back into the kitchen.

As soon as Berry entered the room, he smelled something delicious. Food! He lifted his nose and sniffed the air. The tempting smell was coming from something on the table. Berry thought for a moment. If he could just pull that cloth off the table, the dish might fall on to the floor beside him. He reached up and held the edge of the tablecloth in his mouth.

"Stop!" shouted Mark, grabbing the cloth.

Berry let go and dived under the table, where Bramble was waiting for him.

"Bad luck," Bramble mewed, nudging him with her head. Then she heard a familiar rattling sound. "Don't worry, Berry," she miaowed. "I can hear Mark getting my lunch ready. Crunchy biscuits, yum!"

After lunch, Bramble and Berry curled up together on Berry's blanket and had a snooze. Berry woke up first. He had been asleep for ages, and now he felt full of energy. He jumped up and trotted over to the door. There was a little square flap in it that he hadn't noticed before.

Berry pressed his nose against it and felt his tummy flip over with excitement. He could smell damp grass and leafy trees. The woods! He butted the flap with his head. It swung open, and Berry caught a glimpse of the farmyard through the little gap.

"Bramble, wake up!" he yapped.

Bramble uncurled and sat up. "What's the matter, Berry?" she mewed sleepily.

"I've found a little door," Berry barked. "I think it leads outside."

"That's my cat flap," Bramble mewed. "Watch." She ran over to Berry. Then she stood on her hind legs and pushed her nose against the swinging door. As it opened, she wriggled through the hole. The last thing Berry saw was a flick of her fluffy tail. Then she was gone.

Suddenly, the cat flap swung towards him and Bramble's face appeared. "Come on," she miaowed. "It's easy." Then she disappeared again.

Berry nervously touched the flap with his nose.

"Hurry up!" called Bramble from outside.

Berry didn't find it very easy at all. He pushed and wriggled and scrabbled with his back paws. The sides of the little doorway brushed against his fur. At last he slithered out into the farmyard. But the flap swung back down and hit him on the bottom!

"Ouch!" he yelped, jumping to his paws. Then he stopped. What was that loud roaring noise? Bramble flattened his ears and looked around wildly.

Just then, a big red thing thundered into the farmyard, making the loudest noise Berry had ever heard.

Chapter 4

Bramble watched as Berry shot like an
arrow back through the cat flap. She
bounded after him, and found him
huddled in his blanket. He was trembling
from the end of his nose to the tip of his
bushy tail.

Bramble licked his fur. "What's the
matter?" she purred in surprise.

"Th-that red thing," Berry
whimpered. "It s-scared me."

"It's only a tractor!" Bramble
miaowed. How could Berry be scared

of a silly old tractor?

"W-what's a t-t-tractor?" Berry yelped.

"Mr Gates uses it to ride all over the farm," Bramble explained. "It won't hurt you. Come on."

Berry's paws were still shaking as he left his comfy blanket and followed Bramble through the cat flap again. It was easier to get through this time. Berry was very glad to see that the red tractor was chugging back out of the gate.

"This way," miaowed Bramble as she scampered across the farmyard.

Berry followed close behind her. She led him under the fence and into a wide, green field. Berry felt a shiver of excitement down his back. He had been in this field before. On the far side were some trees.

Berry paused and sniffed. He knew where he was! Those trees were at the edge of the woods where he used to live. Maybe his mum was somewhere in there. He hurtled past Bramble and dashed up the field towards the trees.

"Wait for me!" Bramble called, but Berry was in too much of a hurry.

Suddenly, a brightly coloured butterfly fluttered past his nose, tickling him with its velvety wings. Berry leaped up and tried to catch it, but it flew away. A sweet smell filled his nose. He looked down at his paws and saw lots of little flowers all around him. He burrowed his nose into the flowers and rolled in the grass. The

sun made his fur glow warmly and a
gentle breeze ruffled his ears. It was
great to be outside again!

Just then, he heard Mark calling.
"Bramble! Berry! Where are you? It's
supper time!"

"Yummy!" Berry yapped. "I'm
hungry." He began to trot back down

the field. He looked round for Bramble, but he couldn't see her anywhere.

Bramble had been chasing a baby rabbit. She had followed it right to the top of the field before the rabbit disappeared down a hole. Bramble looked around and realized she was very close to the woods. She could smell lots of exciting scents coming from the trees. "This might be a good place to explore," she mewed, trotting nearer.

She stopped at the edge of the woods and peered through the thick green leaves. It looked rather dark under the trees, but Bramble didn't mind. She felt very brave. With her whiskers twitching and ears pricked, she stepped under the fence and into the woods.

A big, black beetle scuttled across her path. It was smooth and shiny. Bramble reached out to touch it, but it slid under a leaf and disappeared out of sight.

Something tickled her head. Bramble looked up. A spider was hanging from its fine thread just above her. The tiny creature swung to and fro in the breeze.

Bramble was just about to reach up, when there was a strange snuffling sound behind her. She whipped round and pounced.

"Ouch!" she yowled, springing away from the prickly thing. She watched, her eyes very wide, as the spiky ball slowly uncurled. A pointed black nose and two tiny black eyes appeared from the middle of the prickles. Then the strange

animal shuffled off into the bushes.

Bramble shook her tingling paws and decided not to chase after it. She walked further into the woods. A cold breeze ruffled her fur and she shivered. It was starting to get dark. Perhaps it wasn't such a good idea to come into the woods on her own.

"I'd better go back to the farm now,"

she miaowed to herself.

But which way was home? Bramble couldn't remember. She peered round, but all the trees looked the same. Never mind. She would soon find the way.

Bramble squeezed between two large bushes, but she couldn't go any further because there was a very tall tree in the way. She backed out of the bushes and tried another path. It led straight into a clump of very prickly brambles.

Suddenly, a scary hooting sound came from high up in the trees. "Whooo are you?"

Bramble jumped and peered up into the darkness. She couldn't see a thing.

"Whooo?"

What was making that creepy sound?

Bramble narrowed her eyes, but she could only see shadowy branches swaying in the wind.

Bramble realized that she was lost. She crawled under a bush with thick green leaves and thought about home. She began to yowl loudly. "Mum! Berry! Help!"

Chapter 5

It was warm and cosy in the kitchen. Berry crunched up the biscuits that Mark had put in his bowl. When he had finished, he licked every last crumb from around his mouth and nose. Then he looked at Bramble's bowl, which was next to his. It was still full. Where had Bramble got to? She should have been back by now.

Berry trotted to the cat flap and looked through it. It was nearly dark outside. "Bramble!" he yapped. "Where are you?"

He was ready for a nap on his blanket, but he couldn't settle down while he was worried about his friend. He had to go and find Bramble. He jumped out through the cat flap, ran across the farmyard and peered through the fence. He couldn't see Bramble anywhere.

Berry walked into the field and stared up at the woods. The sound of the wind in the leaves made him feel safe. But Berry knew it would be a dangerous place for a kitten at night.

"Oh, Bramble!" he whined. "Where have you gone?" He trotted across the field. "Bramble!" he called a bit louder. "Can you hear me?" He stopped to listen, but there was no answer.

"I'll have to go into the woods to look for her," he yapped.

As he stepped under the trees, Berry lifted his nose and sniffed the familiar woodland smells. A gentle breeze smoothed his fur. He was home!

"Whooo?" came a call from above his head.

Berry looked up. "Hello, owl!" he barked. "I've come home!"

Deep in the woods, Bramble huddled in her hiding place under the bush. She was feeling very scared. The noises of the night seemed to close in around her, rustling and hissing and hooting.

Suddenly, she heard a loud bark not far away. Bramble jumped. Her tail fluffed up and she opened her eyes very wide. What if that was a *grown-up* fox? Now Bramble didn't feel brave at all.

"Help!" she yowled. "I want to go home!"

Berry pricked up his ears. He could hear a faint cry in the distance. "Bramble!" he yapped as loudly as he could. "Is that you?"

Bramble held her breath and watched the shadows. They were full of dark, spooky shapes. Something brushed against her back. She whipped round, but it was only a branch. She pricked up her ears, straining to hear the scary bark again. But all she could hear was a tiny yapping sound. It didn't sound scary. It sounded very familiar.

Bramble sat up. "Berry!" she miaowed at the top of her voice. "I'm here! Help!"

Berry heard Bramble's cry very clearly. "Hooray!" he yapped. "I've found her!" He bounded through the bushes towards the sound. "Don't be afraid, Bramble," he barked bravely into the dark woods. "I'm coming!"

Chapter 6

Bramble sat bolt upright. Berry had come to rescue her! She leaped out from under the bush. "Berry!" she yowled. "I'm over here!"

Suddenly, Berry bounded into the clearing from behind a tree. His fur gleamed like silver in the moonlight. He galloped towards her with his tail stretched out behind him.

On shaky paws, Bramble raced over to him. "Thank goodness you found me," she purred, burying her nose in his thick fur. "It's so scary in here!"

"Don't worry," Berry yapped, licking his friend's ear. "I've come to take you home. Come on." He turned and set off through the wood. After a few steps, he stopped and looked round. Bramble was so close behind, she bumped into his tail. Her eyes were very wide and her fur was fluffed up. Berry felt sorry for her. *The woods must seem very spooky to her*, he thought.

Bramble kept as close to Berry as she could as they trotted through the woods. She couldn't wait to get home. "Thank you for coming to find me," she mewed. "I was really scared."

Suddenly, a dark, slinky shape stepped on to the path. Bramble saw a long,

narrow face and bright black eyes. Sharp
white teeth glinted in the darkness.

Bramble stopped dead. Then she
arched her back and spat. "Berry," she
hissed. "Look out!"

Berry looked up. But he didn't seem
scared at all. Instead, he let out a cry
of delight. "Mum!" he yapped, leaping
up and licking the animal's face. "Where

have you been?"

"Everywhere," barked Berry's mum. She gently nuzzled him with her nose. "I've been looking all over the woods for you. I thought I'd *never* find you."

Berry felt bubbles of happiness fizzing inside him. He had come into the woods to rescue Bramble and now he had found his mum as well! He pushed his nose into his mum's lovely, warm fur and smelled her familiar scent. "I've missed you, Mum," he mumbled.

Bramble watched Berry and his mum making a fuss of each other. She could feel her fur bristling on the back of her neck. It was scary being this close to a grown-up fox! Her teeth looked very sharp, and she was much, much bigger

than Bramble, or even Bramble's mum.
Bramble inched backwards under a
bush.

"Hey, Bramble," yapped Berry,
hurrying towards her. "Why are you
hiding? There's nothing to be scared of."

Bramble crept slowly forward, keeping
her eyes on the big fox's face.

Berry's mum stared down at her.

"Who's this?" she asked.

"It's Bramble," yapped Berry.

Bramble took a deep breath. Her heart was hammering so loud, she thought Berry's mum must be able to hear it. "Hello," she mewed.

Berry ran over to Bramble and pressed his body against her fur. "Bramble looked after me," he explained to his mum. "She cheered me up when I was lost, and she played with me, and now we're best friends."

"Thank you, Bramble," Berry's mum barked kindly. "But what are you doing in the woods at night?"

Bramble went a few steps nearer. "I was exploring," she miaowed. "But I got lost. Berry came to find me."

"And now I'm taking her back to the farm," yapped Berry.

His mum frowned. "We should stay in the woods," she barked. "It's safer for us in here."

"But we ought to take her to the fence on the other side of the field," Berry protested. He wanted to make sure that Bramble got safely back to *her* mum, now that he had found his.

"All right," replied his mum. "But we must take care."

Berry and his mum set off through the woods, following an invisible path between the bushes. Bramble trotted quietly behind them. They soon reached the edge of the trees. Across the field, the lights from the farmhouse twinkled in the darkness. Bramble sighed happily. She couldn't wait to see her mum again, and the lovely warm kitchen. *And* she hadn't had any supper!

She dashed out of the trees and across the field with Berry and his mum racing beside her.

When they had almost reached the

farm, Berry's mum stopped. "Stay here, son," she barked quietly. "We mustn't go any further."

Bramble and Berry banged into each other as they skidded to a halt. They rolled over and over in the long, wet grass.

Berry rubbed his head against Bramble's soft kitten fur. "But Mum!" he whined, sitting up. "I'll miss Bramble."

"I'll miss you, too," Bramble purred. Just then, she smelled the straw from the barn and heard the chickens clucking in the yard. "But I do want to go home!" she added.

"It's time for us to go," barked Berry's mum.

Bramble nuzzled against Berry's

pointed face. "Will you come and visit me again soon?" she purred sadly.

"Yes, lots," Berry promised. "But I can't come into the farmyard any more. It's not safe for foxes."

"And I'd better not go up to the woods again!" mewed Bramble. "They're scary!"

"But we could meet in this field," Berry yapped.

"OK!" Bramble purred. "That's a good idea."

Berry and his mum turned towards the woods, their long tails swishing against the grass.

Bramble felt sad as she watched them slip away into the night. She would miss Berry very much, but she was really glad he had found his mum.

"See you soon!" she called as the white tip of Berry's tail disappeared into the darkness. Then she jumped through the fence and ran towards the farmhouse.

Look out for **Best·Friends** No 6

Blossom and Beany

Blossom the piglet is feeling very sorry for herself. Just because she's small, her brothers and sisters won't play with her! Blossom has to play on her own, splashing around in puddles.

One day she finds a duck playing in her favourite puddle. Beany doesn't think Blossom is too small. In fact, she's the perfect size for a big farmyard adventure . . .

Star the Snowy Kitten

Michael has always wanted a kitten – but his mum says he's not old enough to look after one yet.

Then he finds a tiny black and white kitten in the snow. Star is adorable – but will Michael be able to keep her?

More Jenny Dale titles!

The prices shown below are correct at the time of going to press. However, Macmillan Publishers reserve the right to show new retail prices on covers which may differ from those previously advertised.

JENNY DALE'S BEST FRIENDS

1. Snowflake and Sparkle	0 330 39853 9	£3.50
2. Pogo and Pip	0 330 39854 7	£3.50
3. Minty and Monty	0 330 39855 5	£3.50
4. Carrot and Clover	0 330 39856 3	£3.50
5. Bramble and Berry	0 330 39857 1	£3.50
6. Blossom and Beany	0 330 39775 3	£3.50

JENNY DALE'S KITTEN TALES™

1. Star the Snowy Kitten	0 330 37451 6	£2.99
2. Bob the Bouncy Kitten	0 330 37452 4	£2.99
3. Felix the Fluffy Kitten	0 330 37453 2	£2.99
4. Nell the Naughty kitten	0 330 37454 0	£2.99

All Pan Macmillan titles can be ordered from our website, www.panmacmillan.com, or from your local bookshop and are also available by post from:

Bookpost
PO Box 29, Douglas, Isle of Man IM99 1BQ

Credit cards accepted. For details:
Telephone: 01624 836000
Fax: 01624 670923
E-mail: bookshop@enterprise.net
www.bookpost.co.uk

Free postage and packing in the UK.

Overseas customers: add £1 per book (paperback)
and £3 per book (hardback)